STUDENT BYLINES

STUDENT BYLINES

Anthology: Volume 1

Editors:
Susan Daniels
Seth Vincent

Writers Club Press
New York Lincoln Shanghai

Student Bylines
Anthology: Volume 1

Writers Club Press
an imprint of iUniverse, Inc.

For information address:
iUniverse, Inc.
2021 Pine Lake Road, Suite 100
Lincoln, NE 68512
www.iuniverse.com

Editors:
Susan Daniels
Seth Vincent

ISBN: 0-595-27133-2

Printed in the United States of America

*For all the students who have submitted their
writing and artwork to Student Bylines—thank you
for taking a risk and sharing your creativity!*

"*If you want to build a ship, don't drum up people together to collect wood or assign them tasks and work, but rather teach them to long for the endless immensity of the sea.*"

—*Antoine de Saint-Exupéry*
The Wisdom of the Sands

Contents

Part II   Artwork

Part III   Short Stories

Part IV   Interviews and Reviews

Preface

Student Bylines Anthology: Volume I is a compilation of writing and artwork taken from the first two years of *Student Bylines Magazine*. The premiere issue of *Student Bylines Magazine* was printed in September, 2000 and featured the writing of students in grades six through twelve (with a few exceptions). Entries that were published in the magazine were selected through a peer review process. The magazine was distributed to schools in the Spokane, Washington and Coeur d'Alene, Idaho area.

Countless hours have been spent with the material on these pages—from the first scribbles of an idea in a student's notebook to the binding of the finished pages of this book. *Student Bylines* is a demonstration of the power of a young person's creative voice. The students included in this anthology can be proud to have made a difference by including their contribution and having their voices heard.

It is our hope that a great number of young people will have the opportunity to race through the pages of *Student Bylines* searching for their artwork or writing. When they find their work they will stop…the world will stop…and in that moment they will know the joy of sharing their creativity with others.

To submit your writing or artwork please visit:

www.StudentBylines.com

Acknowledgements

Student Bylines Magazine received support from many individuals and businesses during its first two years of publication. Thank you all for the encouragement and the means to make *Student Bylines* a reality.

Special Recognition

Northwest Images Photography
825 N. Argonne Road
Spokane, WA 99212
(509) 922-0100

Northwest Museum of Arts and Culture
www.northwestmuseum.org
(509) 363-5315

Spokane Teachers Credit Union
www.stcu.org
1-800-858-3750

A heartfelt thank you...

To all the featured authors and artists who shared their expertise:
Sherman Alexie, Terri Austin-Beech, Vicky Cavin, Adrienne C.
Garvin-Dellwo, Caren Furbeyre, Sandra Hosking, Don Kardong,
Rik Nelson, Heather "Ying He" Schwartz, Nicholas Sironka,
Ken Spiering, and Nance Van Winckel

To the teachers who encouraged their students to submit their work
and who shared the magazines with their classes.

To the schools where the magazines where distributed
to the students.

For assistance with advertising, distribution, general office duties,
and encouragement, we express sincere thanks to: Sarah Peterson,
Dan Peterson, John and Wilma Vincent, Shad and Eileen Vincent,
Alexandrea Marvel, and Janet Foulon. Without your effort and support, the magazine would not have made it into the students' hands
each quarter. And to Dan Acree & family—thank you for believing
in and supporting the magazine.

Foreword

Sherman Alexie

I first began writing poetry when I was a student at Washington State University in Pullman, Washington. My first love since way before high school was (and still is) playing basketball, but after being introduced to poetry in a creative writing class, I immediately fell in love with it and quickly became an avid reader and prolific writer of poetry.

Once I started writing I felt unstoppable. I fell hard. Each week, with great anticipation, I would submit dozens of poems to literary journals and magazines. I used a P.O. Box for correspondence, and I clearly remember waiting expectantly by my mailbox for return envelopes from my submissions. When those envelopes appeared I would eagerly grab them out of the box and immediately tear them open. If an acceptance letter was enclosed I became so excited I couldn't contain myself. The people who attended to the mailbox would look at me quizzically and ask me why I was so excited. When I explained, they couldn't understand this joy I felt from knowing something I created would be published.

How could I simply explain my elation? I was only Junior from a small town on the Spokane Indian Reservation, and my creative writing was being accepted for publication in an important literary journal—something I wrote, something I created was going to be circulated in print, with my name on it, for thousands of people to read.

In retrospect, if I had dared, I should have calmly explained to those people at the mailbox that each acceptance letter I received felt like a first French kiss exchanged with someone you've loved for a long time who you've never kissed before.

Read about Alexie's latest projects at www.fallsapart.com.

PART I

POETRY

Challenges of Writing

~By August Wyssman
Eleventh grade, Ferris High School
Spokane, Washington

How can I put into words
just what is in my heart and soul?
Everyday I bare little bits of that soul
to the world, though why I'm not sure
Writing gives me the greatest joy
but also the greatest pain.
I look around my messy room
half-finished stories abound
all over the floor, on my bed, in my closet.
They're everywhere, taunting me
trying to get me to write their endings.
Another sleepless night's begun
with past, present, and future stories running through my
    head.
When I enlisted to do this job,
I never realized the challenges of writing.

I will say one more thing though,
when I see people reading my stories and poems,
and sometimes even enjoying them,
you know something?
Everything makes sense,
and the headaches and the sleepless nights
are all worth it.

Time's Tides

~By Theresa Jackson
Twelfth grade
Philadelphia, Pennsylvania

On the beach
Building castles and eating sandy hot dogs.
Laughing under the umbrella's shade
Being young and free
The children scream in delight
The waves crash up to them and they run away.

On the beach
They belly crawl, dodging bullets
Praying for home, not knowing why they're there
In the first place.
Duty, honor, country, and his girl back home
Waiting for him as the bullet ricochets and his uniform is
    wet.
A lonely hour, gun clenched in hand as he tries to get out
    her name.
Only a gasp.

On the beach
the lovers walk.
Fifty years and still lovers.
Thinking of friends and of the past.
Of how much things have changed.
Arms linked, no hurricane warning tonight.
In the distance children screaming in delight.
How things stay the same
On the beach.

Peace

~By Lissy Metlow
Seventh grade, Valley Middle School
Valley, Washington

A dove
In a sea of vultures,
A candle
In a cell of darkness,
A white horse
In a herd of blackness,
A sea shell
in a hand of sand.

A True American

~By Crystal Orcutt
Eleventh grade, Ferris High School
Spokane, Washington

When a hope or inspiration is found
Find a fault and tear it down.
That's the sickness that's going around.
Here in America
Find a miracle or a saint
Rip it up, graffiti the image with paint.
Distort the purpose make it seem quaint.
Here in America
If a truth is discovered
Change its meaning until it's smothered.
Here in America.
When a politician is elected
Search for the slightest wrong that can be detected.
Here in America.
Build it up, tear it down.
Believe, yet do not claim it.

Be different, yet be more like others.
Trust, yet do not believe one another.
Don't be violent, yet carry guns.
Why? Because it's fun.
To fight, to kill, to be an American:
Killer, peacemaker, warrior, and most of all
Hypocrite.

Beautiful Angels of Earth

~By Ileana Varnam
Ninth grade, Deer Park High School
Deer Park, Washington

When Heaven comes to Earth,
An angel in an exceptional human being,
Our lives change forever,
Everything we see is in a different light.

We do not always see the angel,
It is inside a person,
Not where we can see it at first glance,
Deeper inside is the beauty.

Heaven has no mold for angels,
There is no way that they have to look,
That is why you see no difference on the outside,
Inside their beauty is endless.

Look deeply inside each person you meet,
Treat them with respect,
You never know if the next person you meet,
Is a little bit of heaven.

Mother

~By Christy
Tenth grade, East Valley High School
Spokane, Washington

I could smell the cookies baking in the oven
I could hear the sweet sound of her voice
I could feel the warmth of her touch
How I wish I could see Mother just one more time

A Home Out of Doors

~By Priscilla Thompson
Eighth grade, Homeschool
Rathdrum, Idaho

I would like to live someday in a house of my own
With a lawn that stretches out wide and green
That is thick and moist
To the touch.

Where I can sit, legs crossed, for hours on end
Contemplating the earthworm and the ladybug
With the hot sun beating on my back
During the summer.

It will have trees, tall and wise trees
Stretching their leafy branches up, trying to reach the sky
Where the songbirds twitter
In the shade.

And a garden, full of the sweet scent of flowers and the
drone of bees.
Where I can watch the sprouts grow and spread out
And sift the sun-warmed soil
Through my fingers.

And Cocaine Say

~By Suzanne Miller
Sixth grade, Liberty Lake Elementary School
Liberty Lake, Washington

Sadness in my throat
Sadness in my mind,
And a tear spilling slowly out I find,
I have to think,
I have to wonder,
Who could make such a stupid blunder?
You had the knowledge,
You had the power,
Why did you give in at the eleventh hour?
You were smart,
You were bright,
Now you have no hope in sight.
Now you're dead,
You're gone away,
And it's no one's fault but yours,—and cocaine say.

　　Why?

But you can't answer now.

A Bad Choice

~By Crystal Orcutt
Eleventh grade, Ferris High School
Spokane, Washington

A deep piercing glance.
This is his last chance.
Will he, or not?
Give it all he's got?
A simple apology is all that's needed.
Then she'll ignore the way she's been treated.

Last night was loud.
An old love letter was found.
So as usual he smacked her around.
Again, and again her face hit the ground.

She's got a black eye.
But she dare not cry.
She's going to stay strong.
Besides she was the one who was wrong.

"I'm sorry babe." He pleads.
She forgives him for his bad deed.
Unfortunately he'll forget her pain.
Once his temper's triggered he'll go insane.

Then they'll play this game another time.
What a relationship, with no reason or rhyme.

When will she give up on him?
Her intelligence is growing dim.

She should have left long ago.
But how was she to know?
"He doesn't mean it." She says,
"He hasn't hit me in a few days."

But who's to know he won't tomorrow.
Fill her heart with another sorrow.

Padding On the Banks of Lilly's Stream

~By Lauren Hatcher
Eleventh grade, Ferris High School
Spokane, Washington

The late night air is soft and warm,
A music's in the breeze,
It races through grass and thorn,
And dances in the trees.

It blows past the fireside,
Adding to its spark.
The fair moon showing all its pride,
Its light filling the dark.

A quiet whisper in the ear,
He invites you to run and play.
Nodding to your friend so dear,
Like the wind, you rush away.

This eve there's something special hanging in the air,
You can't quite explain it…But still, it's always there.

My Guardian Angel

~By Jesse Cummins
Twelfth grade, Deer Park High School
Deer Park, Washington

You are my guardian angel.
My one true friend.
When I came into this world
I felt your presence ascend.

You were always able to calm me
When I was being wild.
You acted like an adult
When I acted like a child.

You always had an open ear
To my problems and my pain.
You always knew I was crying
When I hid it in the rain.

My guardian angel's smile
Brightens up my day.
Whenever I am near her
I feel not rage in any way.

My guardian angel protected me
From being filled with strife.
I know not how I could have lived
Without her in my life.

My Dear Great Grandma

~By Twinkle A. Schutt
Eleventh grade, Homeschool
Otis Orchard, Washington

She was my favorite Grandma,
and she will always be,
the one who read me stories,
and said my prayers with me.

She was kind to everyone,
she was a special soul,
whoever you were you got a hug,
and for it there was no toll.

My Grandma had a Music Box,
with Humming Birds inside,
and every time we'd heard it play,
my Dad and I had cried.

This Music Box was different,
sort-of Special in a way,
no one knew just what it was,
not one of us could say.

It played the Unchained Melody,
a song that touched my heart,

and somehow hearing that song again,
made me never want to part.

Eighty-Seven, she'd lived long,
she made it all that way,
then one day she got sick,
so in a Hospital she had to stay.

Then one day as she lie in her bed,
she took her last deep breath,
and now she rests inside the ground,
My Dear Great Grandma, Elizabeth.

Now her house stands still,
'cept the Music Box does play,
the same sweet song and Melody,
it had back in her day.

In Loving Honor of My Dear Great Grandma Elizabeth.
December 27, 1913 to October 7, 2000

J.F.K.

~By Stephanie Guerra
Eighth grade, St. Patrick's School
Spokane, Washington

Waking up to see the sun
Today begins the parade fun

This day, today a time of change
where nothing seems to be in range

The President's car is shined and waxed
for today it will be used its last

When the 60's went and came
a time of love and fame

"Is he ready?" is asked by the murmuring crowd
"He's coming, he's coming!" is yelled so loud

Riding in red so proud
only to be shot exceptionally loud

Near the street
all run with their feet

He falls as the many mourn and cry
only to be found dead in the sky

Right there is where he lay dead
Later, to have flowers hung over his head

gen.

~By Madeline Blodgett
Eighth grade, Chase Middle School
Spokane, Washington

hodgepodge colors swirling dancing million voices still to
    be heard
a generation unsung

screaming endless energy back from heart to heart with no
    belief
a generation unheeded

decadent cruel hypocrites the poison of society
a generation unloved

the future is us but what is our future

Teenage Needs

~By August Wyssman
Eleventh grade, Ferris High School
Spokane, Washington

"Happiness won't get you far"
Or so you've said to me.
You say that I should just grow up,
And forget these silly "needs."

I NEED to be immature at times,
I NEED to be a child.
I NEED to be with my friends,
I NEED to be wild.
I NEED to be a poet, a writer, and whatever else I want to
    be,
basically, what I need,
I NEED to be myself.
So next time that you open your mouth,
bent on crushing a youth's dreams.
Please, for my sake,
Think before you speak.

Thank You

~By Yekaterina Yangolenko
Tenth grade, Colville High School
Colville, Washington

Years have gone,
We have not seen
Nor met for years,
But I have not,
Not at all forgotten you.
You are always on my mind,
Whenever I open my album,
I see you all in smiles
In a blue *Raiders* t-shirt
Standing beside your class
All in smiles.
I remember how I first entered your class
I remember that 1995-1996 school year well,
It was the year my life was turned around,
You taught me how to overcome my shyness
How to fit in.
You welcomed me into your class,
And didn't care about my race.
I would really love to tell you

"Thanks so much,
For everything you taught me
And Everthing you have done in my life."
But the problem is,
I don't know where I could find you.
So I would like to tell you "Thanks"
Through this poem in this magazine.

The Search

~By Gregory W. Hein
Twelfth grade, Davenport High School
Davenport, Washington

Time goes by surprisingly fast,
    It seems as though it was only yesterday.
I just keep looking to the past,
    I wonder why did things have to go that way.

I feel as though I am going blind,
    I cannot even tell where in my life I am going.
Something is missing that I can't find,
    I let something slip away without ever knowing.

I look inside of myself for what I feel,
    What I feel comes from the depths of my heart.
This feeling is so large it's going to spill,
    For with this feeling I just cannot part.

I walk through a maze blinded by light,
    I cannot seem to find the way out.
I am searching with all of my might,
    I seem to be wandering about.

I look to the sky above,
    Suddenly my spirits begin to soar.

I found the answer is love,
    I was looking for the one I adore.

The answer was staring me in the face,
    I finally realized what I had to do.
I walked through the door right out of this place,
    And realized all I was searching for was you.

For Antha In Loving Memory

~By August Wyssman
Eleventh grade, Ferris High School
Spokane, Washington

Bare feet,
A meaningful jewelry box.
A simple ceremony,
A loving send off.

Not on this earth for long,
but in my heart forever.
Some people think it's silly,
But it's the truth.

You shall be missed,
My sweet little water nymph.
Don't forget me, wherever you are going,
I won't forget you, wherever I am.

Guardian Angel

~By Nick Clevenshire
Ninth grade, Jellico High School
Newcomb, Tennessee

The pool is empty with no camper in sight,
I think I am going to enjoy the night.
I watch proudly as you swim to the deep side with a friend,
Glad we are akind.
I say to myself, "If you can, I can,"
I will soon need a hand.
Oh no! You are too far out,
The water is too deep, I can't shout.
At each attempt to yell for help I take more water into my
    lungs,
But why now I'm so young.
That's when I felt a large gentle hand pushing me to the
    surface so I could
yell for help and take a quick breath of air,
You pulled me out of the pool with so much care.

I looked for the person, who had pushed me up to the
    surface,
But there was no one to be traced.
I knew immediately that the large gentle hand was God's
    hand.
You were used as my guardian angel,
So I am proud to say, "That's my sister, Angel."

Dedicated to my sister, Angel, with love.

The Family Room

~By Priscilla Thompson
Eighth grade, Homeschool
Rathdrum, Idaho

The gold wood desk where we've bumped our heads
The couches that we've made into beds
The tables and chairs that have become forts
And burrows and dens and homes of all sorts
The old blue carpet that's turned yellow and green
Transformed into deserts and gardens of queens
The shelves into tall, magnificent castles
Of dragons and ponies with glittering tassels
That room where we spent each childhood day
Losing ourselves and our minds in our play

The Fire at the Edge of the World

~By Priscilla Thompson
Ninth grade, Homeschool
Rathdrum, Idaho

The edge of the world
Caught fire that evening.
The flames grew
Until the whole horizon burned.
The glow spread
Over the mountains that evening.
The drifting clouds were transformed
Into so many velvet butterflies;
Orange and pink,
Lavender and mauve.
The bold streaks of neon
Like long slender dragons
Blended bright light and shadow
On their path to the North.
The last remnant of color,
Deep hot magenta,
Snaked softly away
And left the gray clouds behind.
The fire in the sky died that evening.
Slowly the flame sank
And slipped away to meet the sun
Of some other sky.

The mountains grew cold
And silent that evening.
Standing sentinel over the land.
As the heavens darkened
Into deep shades of gray
The melancholy clouds
Nestled close to the earth.
The Sunset had melted
Into the darkness that evening.
It tip-toed away
As quickly as it had come.

Flakes of Emotion

~By Lee Ciavola
Seventh grade, Saint George's School
Spokane, Washington

Anger, hostility, why are you so,
To take out your feelings in the form of snow.
Summer is grateful, life is good,
But anger reigns, in the cold winter wood.

Spring begins with a joyous sound,
Why freeze the life out of the ground?
The flowers bloom just as they should,
But anger reigns in the cold winter wood.

Fall is old, and crumbling down,
But still lifts her heart, and dismisses the frown.
Now is bare where leaves once stood
And the anger still reigns in the cold winter wood.

Scare away the birds, kill the grass,
What doesn't die, you will harass.
Winter is sadly misunderstood
Anger will always reign in the cold winter wood.

Imagine That

~By Kelly Warner
Twelfth grade, Central Valley High School
Veradale, Washington

What if the sun woke me early one morning?
She would take me in her hand
And place me on a star
And what if a star wanted to impress me?
He would swoop like a bird
And swirl like a cinnamon roll
He would whirl and flutter
Leaving a fiery glow behind him
He would stop momentarily for me to leap to the moon
And what if the moon placed me on his belly?
He would smile and laugh and then he would shake
And what if I began to slide?
He would catch me on his toenail
And drop me on a cloud
And what if a cloud was putting on a show?
It would be a ball then a button then a bird
And what if a bird took me in her beak?
She would spin and swoop and soar about
Then drop me on an ocean wave
And what if a wave wanted to show me the world?
She would place me on her back
And take me for a ride

She would roll past islands unknown to all
Then drop me on a sandy shore
And what if a shore held hands with the sun?
And placed me back where I'd begun
And what if I woke to find it a dream?
I would look to the sky and smile at a friend.

No One Sat on Saturday

~By Hannah Myers
Second grade, Moran Prairie School
Spokane, Washington

No one sat on Saturday.
My best friend
went swimming.
My Uncle Joe went to his shoe shop
where he worked all day.
My Aunt Gloria
went to the beauty parlor
to get her hair done.
But no one sat on Saturday
but me.

Different

~By Mica Smith
Eleventh grade
Manassas, Virginia

You stare at me, I'm not like you
I saw that contemptuous glance you threw,
Over your shoulder, you didn't realize
But, yeah, I saw that too.
Yes, I noticed & No, it didn't hurt
Cuz I don't care,
No, I don't care when you all stare
You laugh at me, mock my style
What are you? Jealous or something?
Get over it.
Don't hate me cuz I'm different.
I don't hate you cuz you're the same
As all the other drones.
You're a robot, programmed to stare,
Brainwashed
While I've got flare.
I'm different & damn proud of it.

I'm flexible cuz I don't care
About the clothes you wear,
The things you do when I'm not there.
So don't hate me cuz I'm not like you.
I'm happy to be just who I am,
& just what I want to be,
Cuz I'm just me.

Confusion

~By Michelle Bronny
Ninth grade, Havermale Center
Spokane, Washington

Offending the molded unconscious.
Borrow a spacious field.
Untouched by the dangling above.
Postured in contorted deals.
Censored for their enjoyment.
Unseen proportions of might.
Idealistic demands ending.
Ending towards unfocused light.

Life

~By Jocelyn Selle
Eighth grade, Valley Middle School
Valley, Washington

I start as a seed
No idea of what is to come,
Needing my gardener's hands to come alive,
To help me survive in this garden of life.
With that help this bundle of life becomes a small sprout,
Fresh and green,
Still naive, inexperienced and dependent.
This life keeps on growing,
Into a young, rebellious and springy sapling,
But, like it or not,
Still needing the stake put behind me to grow strong and
    strait.
As this life keeps on growing,
It becomes a full tree,
Though young,
And still wanting the approving look of the gardener.
This life matures,
And drop seeds of its own,
Full grown independent and strong.

Then,
The life grows elderly,
Sheds its leaves for the final time,
And falls,
Returns to the soil from which it first sprung.

Friendship

~By Katie Peterschick
Ninth grade, Mead High School
Spokane, Washington

Popsicles and baby dolls,
When things were just pretend
Our future was so far away
Remember way back when

Growing up together, always side by side
Friendship through the hard times
I never saw you cry.

My friend; just as a friend
We laugh until we cry
The best out of so many
So many reasons why

My healer; through my eyes
To dry up all my tears
to hold me up and help me
Through these confusing teenage years

My hope is that now you can finally see
How much our friendship had flourished to be

Thank you for the times
Both good and bad the same
And I hope that up in heaven
You will never forget my name.

Sunset

~By Stephanie Wells
Seventh grade, Trinity Preparatory School
Winter Park, Florida

The sun falls to bid good night but leaves just one more
    gift,
Rose pink streaks across the sky smiling back in its bright
    manner.
Did I smile to someone today?

The gentle, blue waves barely crease but arouse to wash
    more shells ashore,
Each one unique in color and style but each stands proud.
Did I accept others for who they are today?

The wind whips through the trees singing its lullaby,
It whispers words of praise for all the quiet listeners.
Did I compliment someone today?

Seagulls soar to their nests but pause to plead for dinner,
An onlooker throws bread into the air as the birds hover
    around.
Did I serve the needy today?

A colorful kite reflects in the sky blowing above the trees,
It swirls and twirls until too dizzy and rests upon the sandy
   beach.
Did I live life to its fullest today?

The stars appear in the evening sky to shine the way for all,
They twinkle for the night and aid the dreamers.
Did I apply my gifts today?

As the last sliver of gold and yellow drip beneath the sea,
I propose my goals for tomorrow and offer thanks because
   I am free.

Sunday

~By Cory Taff
Eighth grade, Colville Junior High
Colville, Washington

The roar of the crowd
The scream of the players
The bash of the pads
The flash of the cameras
    This is Sunday.
The yell of the coaches
The bright lights of the scoreboard
The electricity in the air
The smell of the players
    This is Sunday.
The colors of the jerseys
The discolors of the field
The cheers of victory
The tears of defeat
    This is Sunday.

Morning Changes Into Night

~By Shayla Price
Tenth grade, Thibodaux High School
Thibodaux, Louisiana

In the graveyard of harmony,
the windows fawn,
the doors broaden to peculiar dimensions,
and the serene souls whisper melodies of blissfulness.
My heart drifts into the endless clouds,
Embraced by the passion.
I feel the warmth of the spirits,
But my eyesight is blind to their visual presence.
I'm suddenly enclosed by golden meadows,
On my knees crying.
I can't awaken.
This is not a figment
of my vivid imagination.
The brightness of the sun suddenly changes
into the hours of darkness.
I'm lost in the pasture,
Yearning for the affection of one's heart.
I search for weeks, months, and years.
I still can't find what I lost......
The love of living.

Eyes

~By Alex Ciurlionis
Eighth grade, Glover Middle School
Spokane, Washington

In my dream I watched
They stared each other down
A Demon wreathed in flames
An Angel in white gown.

To forces, good and evil
With the same look in their eyes
The look of true hatred
The look of utter despise.

The Demon stretched his claws
The Angel gripped her sword
The Demon grinned, his teeth bloodstained
As he charged he roared.

The Angels blade flew out
It whistled and it sung
Bright light poured forth
And my eyes burned and stung.

I watched the warriors fight
Fearless and ready to die
Then I woke up in my bed
And stared at the gray winter sky.

Spirits Of The Civil War

~By R. Randolph
Tenth grade, Riverside High School
Elk, Washington

As I walk through the valleys where the Civil War was
    fought,
Where men forgot what they were taught;
I could hear the sounds of guns,
And the sounds of footsteps as cowards run;
The sounds of clashing swords,
The prayers to the Lord;
Between the moans and screams of the injured and dying;
I put my hands over my ears to stop the sounds,
That seem to seep from the ground;
My heart seems to freeze,
As I scream "Be quite, please!"
Then a loud war cry rings out;
And all Charge forth into to certain death,
And the unknown;
I can feel the earth tremble as hooves beat acrossed it;
Then the sounds of scorn,
As people (Normal people) fight over sides;
Forgotten the need for a country unified;
Then the sounds of crying,
As people mourn for loved ones never to return again;
As I feel tears fall from my eyes,

The sounds subside,
As the disturbed ghost who's tales of woe,
Needed to be told;
Finally find the peace so hungered by their souls;
Knowing they're tales will not be forgot;
knowing they got the freedom for which they had fought.

Filled

~By Michelle Bronny
Ninth grade, Havermale Center
Spokane, Washington

A numerous number of feelings consume me.
Feeding the metal rusted water.
Stripped by all awareness,
And melted in a human's mold.
Evaporating the thought of freedom.
Rained upon by other's dreams.
Shaking in confusions winter,
But still remaining unclean.

Fatal Flu

~By Crystal Orcutt
Eleventh grade, Ferris High School
Spokane, Washington

It taught you a lesson. How to be afraid,
and how to understand your life is not a game.
It's more than a lesson, now you can learn no more from
    love.
Even with that wisdom in mind,
There's still that poison in your blood.
How could you lie?
Losing weight, you look afraid, you're scaring me.
I wonder why?
Victim of environment, I cannot stand aside and watch
    you die.
Every day you went to school,
Trying to maintain your cool.
With people sitting far away from you,
No lesson learned.
Here prejudice prevails you're an outcast
To the ignorance of people's mental jails
Soon you'll be free, you can live again my friend.
Darkness is better than this life you live.
Sympathy I give to you,
That is all I can do.
I'm sorry you're stuck here with this fatal flu.

But there's not much I can do.
I guess they taught you the lesson,
How to stay away.
A victim of your solitude and the stress of society.
Now your life's a mess, you should have knew.
Incurable disease, the fatal flu.

Lost Without You

~By K. Clough
Eighth grade, Deer Park Middle School
Deer Park, Washington

On this winding road of life, there are no road signs to tell
    us the

better or easier road to go.

There are no directories or maps.

No hotels to stop and rest at, no guides. Only our friends
    and loved

ones to help us through.

Well, I'll tell you one thing, I'd be lost without you.

New Shoe Blues

~By Jomayra Ivette Torres
Tenth grade, Academy of St. Aloysius
Jersey City, New Jersey

I've got the new shoe blues,
They don't quite fit,
Tried to give ma some clues,
She just told me to sit.
Got the new shoe blues
They're not the right shade,
I liked my old shoes,
The color would not fade.
Got the new shoe blues,
The laces move about,
But not my other shoes,
'Cuz they're all worn out!
I've got the new shoe blues,
Don't like these shoes,
I'll shout and pout,
'Till ma throws 'em out!

Autumn

~By Erica Broadwell
Twelfth grade, North Central High School
Spokane, Washington

The sun rose early
Crisp morning dew was on leaves
The sky was so blue
Not a cloud was to be seen
Colorful leaves here
Colorful leaves all around
Pumpkins on porches
Often people strolled through parks
Among the people;
Children darted to their school
Leaves drifted around
While the sun still shone above
The dew had melted
Pumpkins were being put out
People still strolled parks
Now the children home from school,
Would rake fallen leaves
As the leaves were still falling
It appeared as if
Autumn was fully in bloom

Media

~By August Wyssman
Eleventh grade, Ferris High School
Spokane, Washington

Songs on the radio,
Tellin' me how to be.
People in the media,
Say I'm not good enough as me.
They say I gotta
Buy their makeup
And their TV
All this media attention,
Is gettin' to me.

Earthdweller's Life

~By Liz Blodgett
Eleventh grade, Ferris High School
Spokane, Washington

I am human, love incarnate
Child of God and Goddess pure.
I am made flesh, earth formed to a crude shape
The vessel filled with water of the soul
Hardened in the fire, cooled in the air
Shattered and reformed
Eternally returned.
I am human, sorrow incarnate
Come from the dark side of the moon.
I am ever departing, cold and still.
I am ever returning, warmed by the sun.
I am ever with them
As they are ever in me.
The heat and power of earthdweller's life
Will fade to shadows in their glory.

Friendship

~By Laura Dailey
Eighth grade, Evergreen Jr. High
Veradale, Washington

Friendship is golden
It tastes of the purest sugar
It feels like a warm embrace
It looks like a brilliant rainbow among the clouds
It smells of fresh apple pie cooling
It sounds like the laughter of children at play.

Starry Night

~By Lindsey Kropp
Twelfth grade, East Valley High School
Spokane, Washington

I stared up at the night sky
and saw the stars spread so wide.
They seemed to shine just for me,
even the ones I couldn't see.
I was taken in and swallowed up
and never wanted it to stop.
It melted away all my fears,
their beauty brought me to tears.
I wanted to put one in my pocket to keep
Never had I felt so small and weak.
I didn't want them to go away
But I knew that at the break of day
every last star would disappear.
All I could do is watch from down here
I took a breath and tried to take it all in,
not wanting the night to end.

Ode to a Furball

~By August Wyssman
Twelfth grade, Ferris High School
Spokane, Washington

One summer day,
There I was, typically bored
I got a chance to change the way
My life was being scored.

I got to meet a little dog,
Oh, she was so smart.
I thought I could not have a dog,
But soon, she stole my heart.

To my mother I begged and pleaded,
Sweetly, but with a constant prod.
Until one day she said to be seated,
And said she would consider a dog.

She considered all that a puppy would need,
Like where it would rest, how it would be fed.
Soon enough, days had turned to weeks,
All the while, dreams of the puppy danced in my head.

Finally we knew a puppy's needs we could meet,
And here lies a puppy, sleeping on my feet!

Night

~By Priscilla Thompson
Ninth grade, Homeschool
Rathdrum, Idaho

The moon,
a sliver of pearl
in the quickly—darkening sky,
keeps watch
over the sleeping earth,
glowing as it hangs
in the deep blue sea
of the sky.
The stars,
each a tiny face,
come one by one
into view,
twinkling as the wind
blows across
their little smiles.

The ground,
calm and quiet
in its slumber,
pulls the darkness around it
like a blanket,

sighing softly as it waits
for the morning

The night,
a cool refuge
from the heat of the day,
breathes gently
on those folded
in its embrace,
bathing the earth
with shadow.

And my eyes,
witness to the silent ending
of the day,
hold their breath
and wonder,
looking as if for the first time
at the quiet beauty
of the night.

Fall

~By Justina Long
Eighth grade, Valley Middle School
Valley, Washington

Little kids jumping into a pile of leaves
Their dad just raked
The smell of a fresh pumpkin pie just baked
The little angels and devils that say trick or treat
May I please have some candy to eat?
The crisp pollen breeze
That makes people with allergies sneeze
The leafs on the ground are brown, orange, and gold
And remind us that it will soon be cold
Turkey dinner on Thanksgiving Day,
Is a joyous occasion
Where we eat, dance and play
People will soon need studs on their tires
And lots of wood for their crackling fires
The basketball season is finally here
Its time to hear the fans scream and cheer
Fall is here
It is all very clear
So enjoy it while it lasts
Make it a wonderful past.

Beautiful Still

~By Crystal Orcutt
Eleventh grade, Ferris High School
Spokane, Washington

If I were hung
On the top of the highest hill
Innocence stripped from me
Eyes rolled toward the stars;
If I wore a red gown
that flowed from my head
over my soul to
puddles, lakes, rivers

If I were hung
On the top of the highest hill
With hands crumpled
My neck broken
My lips swollen;
If my skin were exposed
To the taunting night—

Would you hold
Me with your eyes,
Could Beautiful still
Be my name?
Could your fingers again touch

the sides of my face,
would you still gently call to me?

Would you carry me from the hill
Close my eyes
Tear my soul free from the red?
Would tears cut your cheeks
Your voice scream toward
Laughing stars,
Your closest friend become Loneliness

If I were hung
On the top of the highest hill
Would you still say,
"I love you"

Mom

~By August Wyssman
Eleventh grade, Ferris High School
Spokane, Washington

Mom is a special word
And no one else deserves to wear it
Like a beautiful crown upon your head
More than you.
Every day you've taught me something new
Since before I can even remember
You've just got to know I owe my life to you
And I love you more than you'll ever know.

I want to dedicate this poem to my mom. She has done so
much for me, and she's always so willing to do anything to
help me. I love you mama bear!

Skatepark

~By Hope E. Hughes
Ninth grade, Havermale Center
Spokane, Washington

I am there to watch and admire;
They are there always to aspire.

The sound of boards rings out.
He does a trick with no doubt.

Ollies, Nallies, and Kickflips
Sometimes lead to broken hips.

Skateboarder so bold and brave!
Hear the crowd; they rant and rave.

Through good and bad he has his board.
At Skatepark he is lord.

Love Yourself

~By Ileana Varnam
Tenth grade, Deer Park High School
Deer Park, Washington

Media produces,
Picture perfect images.
Pressures everyone,
To strive for impossible perfection.
Find the good things in yourself,
And learn to love them.

PART II

ARTWORK

Dan

~By Seth Vincent
Homeschool
Veradale, Washington

Wolf

~By Corey Anderson
Twelfth grade, Post Falls High School
Post Falls, Idaho

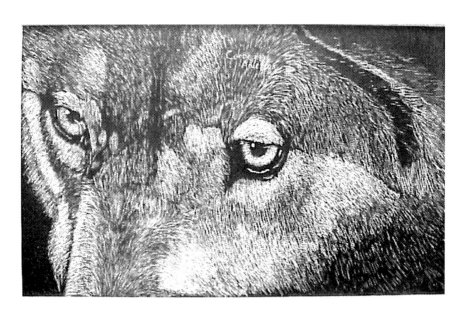

Reflections of Summer

~By Beckie Acree
Ninth grade, Homeschool
Cataldo, Idaho

Blazin' Car

~By Vitaliy Grishko
Ninth grade, M.E.A.D.
Spokane, Washington

Zebra

~By Katie Schultz
Evergreen Junior High
Veradale, Washington

Yellowstone Geyser Basin

~By Shawna Vincent
Reardan Elementary School
Readan, Washington

The Center

~By Jennifer Leader
Twelfth grade, Post Falls High School,
Post Falls, Idaho

School House

~By Anna Marie Schaefer
Sixth grade, Homeschool
Spokane, Washington

Rose

~By Zach De Young
Seventh grade, Medical Lake Middle School
Medical Lake, Washington

Spirit

~By Andrew Morgan
Twelfth grade, Saint George's School
Spokane, Washington

Our House

~By Beau Ferderer
Sixth grade, Homeschool
Spokane, Washington

Balinese Sunset

~By Michelle Vinje
Eighth grade, Saint George's School
Spokane, Washington

Americana Lilies

~By Beckie Acree
Ninth grade, Homeschool
Cataldo, Idaho

Untitled

~By David Porter
Twelfth grade, M.E.A.D.
Mead, Washington

Sunbathing Orchids

~By Gaelen Sayres
Seventh grade, Freeman Middle School
Valleyford, Washington

An Old Friend

~By Priscilla Thompson
Ninth grade, Homeschool
Rathdrum, Idaho

Mango Smoothie

~By Jane Westrick
Ninth grade, Maggie L. Walker Governor's High School
Richmond, Virginia

Scarlet Potentilla

~By Beckie Acree
Ninth grade, Homeschool
Cataldo, Idaho

Seaside Ruins

~By Kim Olsen
Ninth grade, Homeschool
Nine Mile Falls, Washington

Rose

~By Jessica Mann
Eleventh grade, Central Valley High School
Veradale, Washington

Crying

~By Olivia Pearl Distler
Seventh grade, Freeman Jr. High School
Freeman, Washington

Daydream

~By Jane Westrick
Ninth grade, Maggie L. Walker Governor's High School
Richmond, Virginia

Wings of Freedom

~By Tina Green
Tenth grade, Lake City High School
Coeur d'Alene, Idaho

Defense Against Tyranny

~By Alex Fern
Eleventh grade, Saint George's School
Spokane, Washington

Out For A Ride

~By Isabel Cattadoris
Eleventh grade, Reardan High School
Reardan, Washington

Water City: Hope

~By Hector Comacho
Twelfth grade, M.E.A.D.
Spokane, Washington

Getting Froggy

~By Caleb Garrison
Ninth grade, Medical Lake High School
Medical Lake, Washington

The Fishbowl

~By Daniel Peterson
Adams Elementary School
Veradale, Washington

Man & Child

~By Mellisa Lelia Lowe
Ninth grade, Homeschool
Spokane, Washington

Power Within

~By Jennifer Norman
Tenth grade, Gonzaga Preparatory School
Spokane, Washington

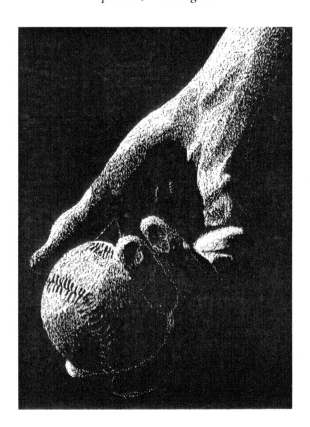

Smokey

~By Ashley M. Lessmeier
Seventh grade, Freeman Junior High School
Rockford, Washington

Bass

~By Gavin Rhodehouse
Twelfth grade, Post Falls High School
Post Falls, Idaho

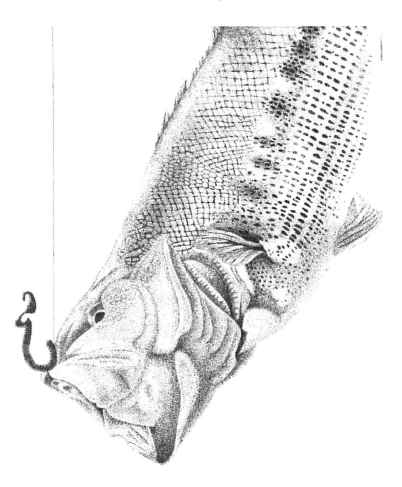

On the Prowl

~By Brandan Drake
Eleventh grade, Riverside High School
Chattaroy, Washington

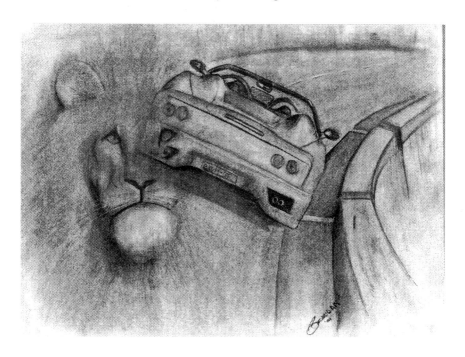

Summer Fairy

~By Ben Barnhill
Seventh grade, Fort Colville School
Colville, Washington

Lizard

~By Elo V. Elwell
Sixth grade, Lakeside Middle School
Plummer, Idaho

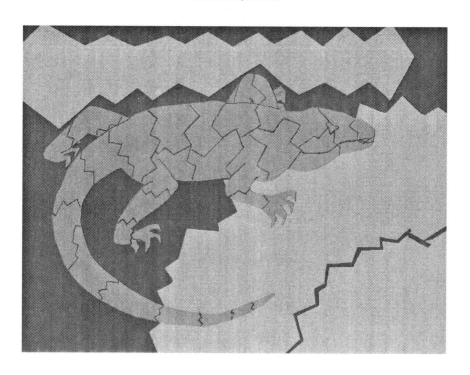

Gone Fishin'

~By Cecelia Jerow
Twelfth grade, Davenport High School
Davenport, Washington

1953 Ford Prostock

~By Taylor Edmonds
Sixth grade, Lakeside Middle School
Plummer, Idaho

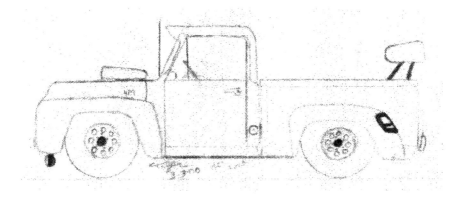

Working the Skill

~By Alex Fern
Tenth grade, Saint George's School
Spokane, Washington

PART III

Short Stories

Rude Awakening

~By Liz Blodgett
Eleventh grade, Ferris High School
Spokane, Washington

And then I woke up. I pressed my fists into my temples, trying to retrieve something, anything, of the night's events.

Nothing.

Here I lie, stranded again, tossed onto a cold, rocky shore by some author's lack of ideas or time.

The last several hours had doubtless been fantastical, even whimsical, God forbid. There would have been humorous side-kicks and gloating villains. There would have been a meaningful relationship with someone whose face would predictably jump out at me as I strolled down the street. There would have been the kind of special effects that give George Lucas heart palpitations. There would have been puns.

And then I woke up.

I thought of calling my friend Jimmy Nondescript to see if he had any advice to give. But then, I knew what Jimmy would say before he even said it. Everyone did. Jimmy was one of those ill-starred creatures, a flat character. He was constantly on call, but never seemed to make it past Chapter Three in one piece. Many long nights I'd spent listening to Jimmy bemoan the luck of protagonists. I never could convince him that probability statistics didn't apply when it came to seven Joe Averages versus one unarmed Dashing Rebel.

Instead of calling, I decided to go for a walk. As I was pulling my long, black, billowing trench-coat on, the phone rang. It was Diana Plot-Advancement, my agent.

"Top o' the mornin' to ya. I've gat a fine and rocking' gig for you, man," Diana told me in her garbled dialect. Diana had worked in Regionalism before coming here and had never gotten rid of the accent. "You want TD 'n' H job? You like?"

"Tall, Dark, and Handsome?" I repeated skeptically. "I don't know, I think I'm getting typecast. Isn't there something fresh on the market yet?"

"You gots da rent to pay, no?"

I confessed that I did. Besides my own room and board, I was also supporting a coquettish yet sinister maid, and enfeebled but gossipy cook, and a surprisingly well-informed gardener who had a talent for being in the wrong place at the wrong time. All of these dependents had been bequeathed to me when dear Papa left me the family mansion. I couldn't really afford it, but I hadn't been able to bring myself to sell the old place. The location was terrible, but at least being at the top of an unpopulated, treacherous cliff meant that Avon ladies were few and far between.

"I'll take the job," I told her, loathing myself for it even as I spoke.

It turned out to be less even than I had expected. Ever since I had gotten my Lurker's License, it seemed like all I did was disappear around corners and meet in taverns to dispense vital and cryptic information. Sometimes I turned evil, sometimes I sacrificed myself gallantly for the cause. I never got the girl. She always went to the supportive and witty noble fellow, preferring sensitive to brooding. They're not the same thing, in case you were wondering.

I came home cursing the industry but blessing the time-and-a-half paycheck that would keep me in hair gel for another week. Certain standards must be kept up, even if only for the sake of appearances.

That's what the whole thing was, I reflected grimly. Appearances. Nobody today wants to bother with story or style. All they want are secretive and cynical characters reflecting grimly in bitter inner monologues.

I flipped on the television in the vain hope of finding something to distract my mind. Watching the characters struggle to fulfill their three-jokes-per-page quota, I felt a strange sympathy arise within me. I didn't envy them, those paper cut-outs on the screen. Trying to mesh the dreams of actors, directors, producers, writers, into a single performance. At least what I did was straightforward. It's a rough job, but somebody's got to do it. That somebody is me.

I'm a character. I do what I do because stories have got to be told. I spit out those clichés you put into my mouth whether they make sense or not, let them roll off my tongue like water off a duck's back. I perform those actions even if they're only inserted because you're getting paid by the word.

I took a moment to stir the embers of the fire with the poker, wondering as I did if it were for the last time.

It's a living. But I'm begging you…make it worth something.

I flipped off the babble box and reclined in the recliner of redundancy. Closing my eyes, I let myself relax and poured the tensions and stresses of literary work into the ground below me.

And then I fell asleep.

I Love You Too, Joey

~By Shannon McDonnell
Eighth grade, St. Patrick's School
Spokane, Washington

This is a story about a boy I once knew. He was my friend and my brother.

When I was about four years old my mother had a little boy. She named him Joseph. I called him Joey. I loved Joey with all my heart and always wanted to be with him, hold him, and play with him.

When Joey was 13 months old he contracted polio. I wasn't allowed near him and being only five years old I didn't understand why. For weeks we thought he might die. Then his fever broke and he began to get better, except his legs, which never did.

When he was three he began to use a wheelchair because he was too heavy to carry all the time. I loved pushing him and vowed to make his life the best I could possibly make it.

When school started I absolutely hated it because I couldn't be with Joey. When school was out I would rush home and do my homework as quickly as I could. Then Joey and I would play, and play, and play.

I remember one time when Joey and I were home by ourselves during a thunderstorm. Joey got awfully scared and was shaking badly. I knew the only way to calm him was to make a game out of what was happening. I told Joey to pretend that we were on a ship (he loved ships) and this bad storm had blown up and we had to save the crew and the passengers. Well, let me tell you, we had so much fun pretending to get the water off the boat and save Ms. Gooden's dog that by the time our mom came home we were laughing so hard that we were crying.

I remember another time when our mom, Joey and I went out to hike down to a nearby creek. We were pushing Joey along when his tire became stuck in a hole. We tried and tried but we couldn't get that wheel out. We decided just to carry Joey. Joey hated to be carried so he asked if he could try to walk. Both my mother and I knew he couldn't walk, but my mom said he could if he wanted to.

Amazingly, Joey proved us wrong. He took one step and then fell down. From that day on Joey would brag all over town about how he had taken one step.

Joey had his ups and downs. On his down days he would become very stubborn and would refuse help from anyone. I would become frustrated and would want to yell, but reminded myself that this life was very hard and I needed to work with him.

His up days were when he was willing to be helped and would cooperate. His big up days were when someone would say to him, "Well, son, I overheard that you took a step on your own, why don't you tell me about it."

He had the most fun telling that story to the people in the town. He would tell it to the men outside the barber shop and all the men would watch him as if he were worth a million dollars and to us he was worth much more.

Since we lived in a small town everyone knew who Joey was and everyone loved Joey, but it wasn't always that way.

When Joey started kindergarten our mother told Joey that some kids might make fun of him and that he just had to tell them why he was in a wheelchair and that he just wanted to have fun and make friends like everyone else.

Well, there was one boy who made fun of Joey. His name was Billy. Billy made fun of Joey as soon as Joey cam in. Joey calmly explained why he was in a wheelchair and that he was no different than anyone else.

Billy, mesmerized, asked if he could push Joey and from that day on wherever Joey was, Billy was there too and wherever Billy was, you could find Joey too.

Joey loved life and lived it to the fullest.

When I was 17 years old and Joey was 13, he became sick and the polio disease finally took his life.

He fought as hard as he could, but in the end he realized this fight was much too difficult even for him.

On the day he died he whispered to me, "Jayme, thank you. Thank you for giving me the best life I could possibly have and teaching me to reach for my dreams. I think I had a lot more fun in the wheelchair. I love you, Jayme."

"I love you too, Joey"

As soon as I had said that Joey died. That was the hardest day of my life. I cried all day.

Five days later we had his funeral. The town lined the streets to say one final goodbye to Joey.

Joey was buried with two objects: a baseball that he and Billy used to play with and a picture of Joey and me. It was his final wish.

I'm telling this story because Joey deserves it. He learned to live life to the fullest even though he was in a wheelchair. I hope that in reading this story you will learn to live life to the fullest.

I love you, Joey

Dedicated to my Uncle Robin, with love.

The Beauty of Life

~By Briana Bryant
Eighth grade, CMIS
Chang Mai

The rough wood scrapes against my bare legs as the silky breeze flows into my nostrils and caresses my body. I catch the rusty chain of the swing and push off into the fair turquoise sky.

In my mind, I fly! High up in the sky with the sun soaring and screaming colors of magenta, lemon, and tangerine. The wind whistles a tune to me, a sweet lullaby that tickles my ears and tells of days long gone, and days to come. Time does not belong in my world. I am all alone, lost in the icy sea of my thoughts. Only the essence of just *being* courses through my body, of *being* me. Only the fuzzy feeling of warmness, the last hug from a loved one.

I collapse on the grass by the tree and look at the fluffy misshaped clouds that smile down on me. A tiny bird tweeps in its nest, and a smile creeps over my face as a dainty buttercup grins up at me, its mellow butter alighting my face with sunshine. Its slender stem moves lithely, dancing and swaying to the rhythm of the breeze. All of nature joins in, and as I stare in wonder and awe, I realize something—that we are all part of a beautiful waltz, the music pulsing in our blood, the ballet of milky swans, the tango of the frogs…And each person dances life to a different rhythm, a different beat.

As the pale pink pastel of dawn awakens life, the shimmering rays of sunlight fall like fiery droplets of rain in a halo around me. The sun eagerly begins its many long hours of careful nurturing and feeding, as a mother cares for her young.

The dew dropped apple grass turns golden in the morning light, and the swing stands abandoned, the picture of solitude and reflection, swaying softly back and forth, as a leaf falls gently, carried to its resting place by the wind.

A place of peace, and rest, of introspection and quiet. A place where God is found, in the leathery bark of the tree, in the melody and song of the robin, and in the wild flowers that are independent, free, and have no worries…A place where I can just be ME.

Old Hands Make Beautiful Art

~By Jeremy Trimble
Tenth grade, Foothill High School
Rio Linda, California

As I ran the perimeter of the enormous park I could feel it push me. I didn't understand what it was so I ran. It lurked in my brain, or maybe in my soul; it was strong at that moment. It shoved me forward granting my legs strength I didn't know they had. My crisp jog in the cold morning air slowly transformed into a full sprint.

Before I could understand what was happening my legs were becoming more stubborn. Momentum stored in my legs refused to allow me to slow. It was then that I finally realized what was going to happen. In front of me, only a short distance that was rapidly shrinking, an older woman was sitting in a chair. I didn't notice it then but there was a table in her lap; creatures of her imagination were being created on the yellow pages.

I couldn't stop. I realized I had a choice: I could run that poor woman down or I could move over to the side a little and trip myself into the grass. By then my breath was shorter than I might have liked. If my brain had received an appropriate amount of oxygen I'm pretty sure I could have simply gone around her and let my momentum slowly fade. I didn't think of that.

I altered my course slightly. Old sneakers stuck to my feet began pounding against the vibrant green grass. As motion went on I forced myself to stop, one leg took a step and I didn't let it move again. My body crumpled forward slamming into the soft earth.

"Are you all right young man?" a voice asked. The thin layer of sweat that coated my body quickly betrayed me to the bitter air. Suddenly shivering I pulled myself up, angry with myself, and the stupid woman who caused me to trip.

"Yeah," I answered briskly. "I'm okay," I was gracious, "Are you hurt?"

"No," she responded with a slight smile, "You could have gone around and slowed down. I didn't think sitting in the middle of the path would cause so much—disturbance."

A flash of anger surged through me. "Yes, I'm sure you didn't," I conceded. Honestly, frustratingly, and logically I continued, "It's early still, most joggers won't be out for a while."

"That is what I believed."

I stood up and noticed the yellow tablet. The thing in my head suddenly pulsed to life again. I could understand it a little bit more then. It felt like an unknown desire. I guess it would be like birds' desires to fly south for the winter, or for salmon to swim upstream in their season. This desire, I guessed, tugged at me. I didn't know what it wanted. I used it to run, and run well, but was it more?

"You're hurt," she declared. Her face crinkled slightly. Only then did I notice the myriad of lines and wrinkles that gave this woman a sense of distance. It was like she had seen a great deal more than I ever could. Her long silver hair seemed to match the slight smile she wore.

I looked down at my right leg and saw a long bleeding streak of crimson fluid. Noticing it must have awoken the sleeping wound because it suddenly decided to wash me in frustrating pain. "It's not so bad," I finally said after a slight flinch.

"I live across the street," she pointed to a white house, "come over and wash that wound. That ground isn't as clean as it could be."

I nodded and was about to decline as politely as my frustration would allow when she suddenly turned around with her tablet in hand and began walking across the street. I followed, hesitantly after several heartbeats. She was unfortunately right. Besides, in retrospect I think that desire that throbbed in my head wanted me to go. As it pushed my legs into a stupid sprint, it urged me to follow this old woman who seemed kind.

We quickly made it across the street and to her front door. She opened the door and I followed. "By the way," she said, "my name is Sara Jennings."

"I'm Jeremy," I replied shortly. As we came into the first room the sheer beauty surprised me. The walls were covered in pictures of the abstract, animals, places, and people. There were pieces that held nothing more a few colors creatively splattered onto canvas. Others were drawings that could have been colorless photos. One piece caught my attention and held it.

A rose sat on a piece of paper. It was framed, almost entrapped behind the glass. The lines were perfect, and the coloration was unique. My eyes were focused on the little plant for a long time. It was hypnotic.

Ms. Jennings returned and handed me a damp cloth. I sat down and began dabbing the gash. The warm fabric sheet felt comforting against my wound. Each time I withdrew the cloth it was stained red, ironically the exact same shade as the rose that still tugged a little at my gaze.

"Where did you get these?" I wondered aloud.

"I made them, I'm an artist of some small talent."

"They are very beautiful," I stated emphatically. They were.

"Would you like to learn how?"

The desire in my mind suddenly bloomed like a flower feeling sunlight for the first time. I quickly said yes and at the moment she walked out of the room and returned with a few pieces of paper and pencils.

I tried to draw. I failed. She showed me several techniques, and I learned those readily enough. I tried to draw again and I failed again. Frustration began clawing it's way back into my mind.

"Be patient. I'll tell you something about my artworks," she leaned closer to me like she was sharing a deep secret, maybe she was. "I couldn't draw until I saw something very special to me. It was a moment of understanding and revelation.

"You see that," she pointed to the rose, "I saw that in a park once, I knew I had to draw it and I drew it. Later I colored it, but the first good piece has to be something special, something of the greatest beauty."

The words ingrained themselves in my mind. Later I had to leave, but I did return to learn that I'd made a friend with Ms. Jennings. She taught me different disciplines of drawing, painting, coloring, and a dozen different art forms.

Not so long ago she died. I went to her funeral.

The coffin was open. Her gray hair was neatly arranged. Her face still seemed to hold that slight smile. A smile spread across my lips. I was sad to see her gone, but I knew she had lived her life as an artist.

Then I noticed her hands. They were on her chest, criss crossing one another. A revelation flashed through my brain, or maybe my soul. That little tugging in my mind pulled harder. Once the funeral was over I sprinted home knowing what I would draw. The drawing of two aged hands crossing each other is still hanging on my wall.

Old hands that created so much beauty should be remembered. These venerable hands made beautiful art. Ms. Jennings taught me art while her hands help me remember.

Day Dream Of Doom

~By Matt Greer
Twelfth grade, North Central High School
Spokane, Washington

"Man this bus ride is boring," Mike said. "I don't know if I can stand three more hours of this. There is no leg room, the people on the back are too noisy, and there's nothing interesting to look at out the window" Mike said.

"Pipe down," yelled the bus driver.

Mike sighed as he gazed out the window. Suddenly he saw a giant floating TV set. As he looked closer he saw what was on the TV set. It was him riding the bus. "Bah," he said as he snapped back to reality, "even my imagination is boring."

He gazed out the window again looking at the endless wheat fields. In the distance he noticed something. He couldn't make out what it was, but it was huge and it was headed towards the bus. As it got closer Mike realized it was a giant turtle. "Whoa, it's Gamera!" Mike exclaimed. The turtle got closer and closer until it was less than half a mile from the bus. Mike watched in awe as it screamed loudly and crashed through the wheat fields. As Gamera neared the bus Mike felt a fear rush through his body. Finally Gamera was at the bus. It turned it's head toward Mike's window. Suddenly, fire shot out of it's mouth and headed toward the bus.

"The wheels on the bus go round and round, round and round, round and round," some kids in the back sang loudly. Mike was snapped back to reality.

He gazed back out the window but saw nothing but some cows and farm houses. Mike reached under his seat into his bag and pulled out a book to read. As he sat reading he paused from his book and looked out the window and saw Gamera again. Gamera was charging toward the bus at an incredible speed.

Just as Gamera was about to reach the bus, Godzilla appeared and knocked Gamera down. Just as Godzilla was about to finish off Gamera, Moth-ra flew in and knocked Godzilla down. And just as Moth-ra was about to feast on Godzilla, Oprah Winfrey showed up wearing a bib and holding a fork and knife. All the Japanese monsters fled in panic.

Mike turned his head to look out another window and he saw giant transparent letters bouncing around forming random words. "What is this?" Mike asked. The giant transparent letters answered him by spelling out THIS IS THE END OF THE DAY DREAM OF DOOM!

Griffey's Home Run

~By Julian Redman
Sixth grade, Post Falls Middle School
Post Falls, Idaho

It is a searing hot day at Safeco Field in Seattle, Washington. The sun is blazing in the crystal blue sky like the yolk of an egg. On this boiling, fiery day, the Seattle Mariners face the New York Yankees in the World Series. With the Yankees in the lead, the score is 11 to 8. It is the bottom of the ninth. The Mariners are up. The bases are loaded. Last inning, last batter, last out. On first base is Edgar Martinez, on second is Alex Rodreguez, third base is Jay Buhner, and up to bat is Ken Griffey Jr. The batboy emerged from his seat in the dugout to home plate with a armload of bats. Griffey calmly selected a black bat and walked to the plate. The Yankee pitcher Mike Santon gave Griffey a nasty smirk. A trickle of sweat trickled down Griffey's face. He nervously gripped the bat just as the ball ripped from the hands of the pitcher. Griffey gave all of his might and swung, but all he heard was the ball slam into the catcher's mitt and the umpire yell, "Strike One!"

The catcher hurled the ball back to the smiling pitcher. The trickle of sweat returned once more to Griffey as he gripped the bat. The pitcher threw the ball and Griffey swung hard.

Crack!

He belted the ball into section 112. He could hear the squeals of delight from a six-year-old youngster who had retrieved the ball. Griffey ran to first, jogged to second, sprinted to third, and finally slid home where his teammates congratulated him with high fives.

Two overwhelmed players picked up the ice cooler and dumped its contents on their excited coach. Griffey took the pennant and held it high over his head. Tears of joy had replaced the trickle of sweat. The Yankees grabbed their gear and sulked out of Safeco Stadium. The score board now read 11 to 12, Mariner's win!

There's Something Under the Rug!

~By Sarah Peterson
Seventh grade, Evergreen Jr. High
Veradale, Washington

One rainy and stormy night a man named Bob and his wife, Bethany, were going to the mall. Right when they were about to leave, Bob saw something move under the rug.

"Beth, honey, come here quick."

"What is it Bob?" Beth asked.

"Look, there's something under the rug."

"Bob, I'm scared!"

"There's nothing to be afraid of," said Bob. Then, with a thud, it knocked down the table and lamp.

"Not my table and lamp!" Beth yelled.

"I'm going to try to get it." Bob said.

"No Bob, it's probably just a mouse. Let's go and have fun at the mall."

"You're right Beth. Let's go to the mall."

Two weeks later…

When Bob and Beth were just about to go to bed, Bob said, "Beth come here and hurry. The thing that was under the rug two weeks ago is back! We need to find out what it is,"

"We?" exclaimed Beth. "I can't do anything about it!"

"We have to Beth, now come on."

"All right, all right, I'm coming." sighed Beth.

"I think the thing under the rug is a rat." stated Bob.

"A rat!" exclaimed Beth. "I hate rats. They're so disgusting."

"I know, I know, but the sooner we get rid of it the better." said Bob.

"Okay, let's go to Fred Meyer. It has everything." suggested Beth.

Two hours later…

"I hope that thing is still here," said Bob.

"Bob, your wish came true, but now there are two of them!" shouted Beth."

"Two of them! Well, we need one more box of the poison. Beth you go to the store and get some more. I'll stay here with the lumps," said Bob.

"Okay, I'll be back in about ten minutes."

"Okay, hurry!" Bob said as he helped Beth out the door."

Fifteen minutes later…

"Bob, I'm back!" shouted Beth.

"Oh, thank goodness you're here! I've been trying to tie these things down," said Bob. "Now it's your turn."

"I don't think so mister," replied Beth. "Look Bob, they stopped moving. They must have bumped their heads on something."

"That's great, now we can see what they are," said Bob.

"On the count of three let's lift the rug, okay?" Beth suggested.

"One…two…three…"

"Meow, meow."

"Look Bob, they're just cats. They're so cute."

"Yeah, we better put up a flyer saying that we have two cute, lost cats in our home." said Bob.

"Yeah, I guess you're right."

A Monster Lives Under My Bed

~By Caroline Stephanie Kraft
Sixth grade, Homeschool
Elk, Washington

It all started when my mom left the living room door open. That's how the monster came in. He looks like a big ugly lizard with sharp teeth. I haven't seen him, only his shadow. Sometimes I don't see him, but I know he's there at night, after my mom tucks me in bed. I always turn on the light to read and there he is. I'm not sure if I should be scared of him or not. All I know is, I want him to go away.

Whenever I tell my mom, she says it's my imagination, But someday I know he's going to come out from under the bed and I don't want to be there when he does. I hate him! When I have people staying the night, he scares them by showing up. After that, none of my friends want to stay the night. I hate that stupid lizard thing, he is ruining my life! I think he is going to be here for a while. He's been here for two weeks and still hasn't gone away.

One day, I went to school and found out my friend Tom had started a rumor. He said that I had a huge animal under my bed and that he eat's people. I was enraged! Inside, I knew that I did have a monster under my bed, but he had never eaten anyone.

That night, I was laying in bed and turned on the light to read. He was back! After two weeks of living in fear, I wanted to see what the horrible thing was. All of a sudden, I heard scratching. I imagined the monster was trying to get to me. Trembling with fear, I peeked over the edge of the bed and gently lifted the blankets. There it was, my horrible monster. But, instead of being a big ugly lizard, he was a cute baby lizard! Instead of being my monster, he was my pet.

In the morning I went to school and showed everyone my monster. They all laughed at the sight of him. Later that night my friend Tom called and said he was sorry for the rumor he started. My Mom and Dad said they were sorry for doubting me, and said I could keep my new friend.

My Dog Tess

~By Julie Baxter
Eighth grade, Evergreen Jr. High School
Veradale, Washington

"What the heck was that awful noise?" It was a Saturday morning. I was awakened by the shrill howling of my beagle, Tess. I sat up in bed knowing that, no matter what, I'd never be able to go back to sleep. Trish yelled up to me, "Shut your dog up. Some people are trying to sleep!" I ran downstairs only to find my dog's bottom stuck in the dog door. She was trying to scare away something that wasn't even there. This was a daily routine with her.

While my dog was busy howling (at nothing), I started to untie my shoe. Once untied, I picked up my shoe and threw it at her. I know, I know, that was mean, but I couldn't yell at her. I didn't want to wake anyone else up. After throwing the shoe, she jumped through the dog door, turned around, and jumped back through. She looked at me as if to say, "Kid, you hit me with your shoe? Well, okay I'll just have to take it then." She then picked up my shoe and ran outside.

Then, with me staring out my window watching my dog, I wondered what she was going to do to my helpless shoe. She stopped in the middle of the yard and turned around in a circle three times. When she stopped, she began to run the perimeter of the yard with my shoe still in her mouth.

Later, when Tess had stopped to catch her breath, it started to rain. Since I didn't want my shoe to get wet and torn to shreds, I crawled through the dog door looking for Tess. I caught her lying under the slide, and do you know what she was chewing on…That's right MY SHOE! I walked cautiously, not wanting to get Tess into an endless run. Just then I had to step on a dry leaf. CRUNCH! Tess jumped up at the alarming sound. I was never going to catch her again.

It was the next day. I woke up by my dog's squealing howl. I knew once again that she was howling at nothing. This time, instead of getting dressed, I picked up my shoe and walked downstairs, I was aiming my shoe at my dog's bottom. I know what you're thinking, she'll just take my shoe again. Not this time, I think she learned her lesson. WHAM!! Wait TESS, give me back my shoe. It was happening all over again.

A Different Wheel

~By Divya Vishwanath
Seventh grade, Saint George's School
Spokane, Washington

I looked into the twinkling, curious eyes of my only granddaughter. The dark chocolate pools glistened against her fair skin. I only wished her eyes could stay innocent and carefree forever.

"Grandmama, what is racism?" Silence filled every corner of the bedroom, sweeping over the two of us. I remember asking the same question in my childhood.

"Well…" my voice creaked, "Racism is unfairness in mankind. Racism is…" I tried to dissolve back in time to my very own grandmama's wrinkled face. How the corners of her eyes crinkled when she smiled. Her words came to me. "Racism is a giant color wheel, in which colors are all that matter." I slowly surfaced from the bed and the closet creaked as I pulled the brass handles. I pulled out a box. It had a rusty old front, and dust speckles grew on the top. I pulled out an old piece of parchment. I began to read:

> "If black is black and white is white,
> Are all hearts made of stone?
> Do we know what's wrong or right?
> Someone must have known?
>
> Before white became the top,
> On the curious color wheel,

Couldn't someone stop?
Before it's hurt we feel?

Do not fear young one,
For world's are starting to learn,
The moon, the stars, the sun,
It's peace that we may earn.
Peace that we may yearn."

My grandmama's face disappeared and I looked at my grand-mama's cramped writing. I stared at my grandchild, and tears began to drizzle down my cheeks.

"Do not cry, Grandmama, do not cry." I watched as this proud African child stared at me defiantly. "I will make a difference!" She cried, "I will make a difference."

Being Small

~By S. Jackson
North Central High School
Spokane, Washington

Everyone gets called names at sometime in their life: tomboy, sissy, four eyes, metal mouth, klutz, etc. But then the victims of this juvenile verbal abuse grow up. "Tomboy" becomes Lilac princess, "sissy" becomes a linebacker, "four eyes" gets contacts, "metal mouth" has beautiful teeth, and "klutz" becomes a ballerina. But when you're short and grow up, you don't necessarily grow up. We get called "shorty," "pint size," "squirt," "shrimp," and "pipsqueak," sometimes all our lives. Even though many people say we are "cute," being short sucks because you struggle through daily life, basic maneuvering, and participation in some sports.

Being small makes daily life a relentless struggle. First of all, you look younger simply because of size. Can you imagine how it feels to be able to drive to a restaurant and still get asked if you want a kid's menu with crayons? And there are clothes too. It's choice between shirts and pants that don't fit that are from the junior's department or hot pink shorts and Winnie the Pooh shirts from the children's department. Then there are seats. It's quite easy to get sick of sitting in seats where your feet don't touch the ground. Plus, you're always volunteered to sit in the middle when riding in a car with your friends. Oh, and don't forget school. You can't reach some shelves; you get stuffed in lockers or canned and you're always in the front row for everything. Just your basic day-to-day activities are difficult for us.

What is most troublesome is basic maneuvering—getting from one place to another. The most difficult part is getting through crowds. Have you ever played pinball? Do you remember how the ball bounced from side to side endlessly? Now imagine you are the ball. That is how it feels to be in a crowd when you're at least six inches shorter than ninety percent of it. Dealing with our crowded halls about seven times a day is a struggle, especially when your backpack weighs more than you do. Then there are the little things, like having training wheels until you're twelve because you could never reach the pedals; or having pillows on the car's driver seat because otherwise you can't see above the steering wheel or reach the pedals. You can't see over people at movie theaters or anywhere for that matter. Even band is more difficult. Have you ever seen a small person play the tuba? I can tell you from experience that marching is hard when your instrument hits your knees and cuts up your face. Basic maneuvering can prove to be quite a challenge, along with other activities.

Sports is a common challenge for the vertically challenged. Popular sports like volleyball, basketball, and bowling can send small people into hysterics at the simple thought of attempting any of these "regular-size" oriented events. For example, in volleyball, you should not be able to stroll casually under the net. In basketball, the ball should be passed to you, not over you. And in bowling, the ball should not weigh more than fifty percent of your body weight. Even small things like uniform size and glove size for softball have an impact. You should not trip over your uniform when running bases or have your glove fly off when trying to catch a ball. Being small makes participation in sports extremely tough.

So when you get down to it, being small sucks. It is hard to get through each day, get around, and take part in sports, but hey that's life. Because of our petite size we are often "overlooked." Many assume that we are shy and innocent because they relate size to childhood. This assumption is based on plain ignorance. So next time you speak to a small person, don't feel sympathetic—because they can stand tall, in a matter of speaking, and converse with you as if you were "eye to eye."

Rolling into Life

~By Rachel Marie Lewis
Twelfth grade, Rogers High School
Spokane, Washington

Once you start the journey into life you begin a ride that can seem like an eternity; however, it can pass by like a blink of an eye. For life is a roller coaster. It has it's up's and down's, twists and turns. You can live high or live low. Life can continue on, and can become a repeating cycle, so much like a roller coaster. This ride has a beginning and will also end in sometime or another, but this ride you will never forget. They have their fond memories of being in delight, frightened or in utter disgust, and sometimes it can just make you feel sick. One cannot predict what may happen next, life can only run its course over time. We learn to live together, but we die alone. It's like riding the roller coaster with others, but you get off the ride alone. You really don't know where you are going, but you remember where you have been. At one point or another it can make you change your direction in life, but unlike a roller coaster a person chooses the direction it may lead them. At times you can remember certain aspects or events from the past, a reminder of what you are really here for. We all enjoy this ride, and want to come back for more.

Everybody sit down, strap yourself down, and hold on tight for you are on the ride of your life!

PART IV

INTERVIEWS AND REVIEWS

An Interview: Mel McCuddin

~By Katy Brukardt
Tenth grade, Lewis and Clark High School
Spokane, Washington

I gingerly approached the front door of a small house, notebook in hand. What would he be like? My parents had told me he was as interesting as the mysterious artwork that he painted, and when I first saw his smiling, weathered face greeting us and telling us to follow him to his studio, I knew immediately that I liked him. We crossed the stone walkway through a backyard studded with iron sculptures and glassworks, toward a small studio in the back. From the outside, the wooden building seemed like any other, but inside held the scent of inspiration and creativity. The speckles of paint framing Mel's easel hinted at hundreds of painting that had come to life through his brushes. Some of them still lingered around the room; a sullen monkey rested against the wall on the floor, the eyes in the painting immediately grabbing my attention.

"That one looks like a couple of people that I know," commented my mother, and I knew she meant my sister and me. My father and I laughed.

"I call that one 'The Pouting Primate,'" Mel offered. I tried to observe everything in the room at once, without turning my head, which proved impossible. Masks and paper kites and pictures of animals decorated the walls. There were several paintings—a fish, a deer, three wobbly men—but most interesting of all wasn't what already had been created, but what remained in the process.

Pulling out a painting in progress, the artist explained, "First, I put a lot of paint on a canvas." The wash of colors shouted like a playground of children with boundless energy. It didn't resemble the finished paintings I remembered seeing, and I eagerly anticipated how he transformed something like this into a mournful cow or, well, a pouting primate.

"It's kind of like looking at the clouds," he continued, and I imagined myself gazing into the sky creating objects from the billowing white clouds above me. "I look for shapes, and then I outline them, filling in the background around them and leaving the original canvas to show through. I never think about what I'm going to create before I do my paintings, and that's one of the things that I like about art. When I do art, it's exciting because I'm the first one who has ever seen it."

I recalled the time when my grandfather showed me a peanut, still in its shell, and told me that we were the first ones ever to see that peanut. Then he popped the nut into his mouth saying, "and no one will ever see it again!"

We found ourselves following Mel into his house—a museum of art in itself, with the walls covered with paintings by fellow artists—down into his basement, where canvas upon canvas waited to be discovered, like so many archaeological bones. To my young eyes there appeared to be enough to have taken his whole life to paint, but he assured me that despite his love of art, he hadn't always painted. In fact, he used to be a truck driver, and when he returned home late at night after work was when he nurtured his creative genius. To this day he works mostly in the evenings, out of habit.

"When I was a kid," Mel began as he invited us to look through the paintings resting on the floor, "my parents went to a carnival, and bought one of those paintings done with a big brush. I remember looking at it and thinking, 'Now that is something I could do!'" As picture after picture clacked together, I agreed that, indeed, painting was something he could do. As we prepared to leave, I asked him whether he would like to do anything else in his lifetime besides painting. He chuckled and replied that nothing could replace art in his life. "I believe everyone has to create something to be a complete person."

I left that afternoon itching to splash paint onto a canvas, pulling human emotion out of each color and shape, just like Mel. Spokane is fortunate to be home to such an individual, who can enrich everyone around him with his art and his creative mind.

A Life Worth Living

~By Kim Adams
Freshman, University of Washington
Seattle, Washington
Graduate of Mead High School

My uneasy eyes follow his ghostly body as he silently wanders through the frenzied crowd and anxiously searches for a place to hide. He drops his head shamefully, and gently pulls the bill of his ragged Mariner's cap tightly over his wild and untamed locks. Reality whispers in his ear and tells him that his life is just as worthless as the withered baseball hat. Like a feeble and injured prisoner, he believes if he is unnoticed he may have a chance of survival.

The hot cafeteria food is hoggishly crammed into his hollow stomach followed by loud screaming slurps of juice. Gossiping girls nearby cringe, and pull their trays away in disgust. He sits alone because they say he is different. He does not react to the staring eyes because he is accustomed, and understands he will not eat until this time tomorrow. He continues to hover over his sacred dish and frantically fills his aching belly, for he is aware of the ticking clock.

I secretly cheer him on with hopes that he may take one more bite because soon the torture will begin. My heart sinks. The enemy has already spotted him and snakishly approaches the victim fully informed of the victim's inability to prepare for this daily war. The hateful words fly from the enemy's numb and careless mouth like bullets and scars the victim with wounds that may never heal.

I squeeze my eyes shut, hoping the pain might find an end, but even the enemy is unable to see the consequences of his thoughtless acts. The enemy's sinful ignorance severely blinds the enemy from morality and truth. The victim cries out, but no one seems to listen or care. Every mocking slur and degrading phrase kick me in the gut, and I can no longer fathom to except this maltreatment. No longer will I watch these demented scientists dissect the human spirit.

Yes, I tell the authoritative figures, but they cannot mend a broken soul. Every person has a soul, but his is shattering and growing cold and dark. He has been beaten and scarred, both mentally and physically. He has been brutally outcast by a young society who savagely and greedily crush those who may get in the way of popularity. He is exhausted and frail.

Through this experience, I have learned the affects of severe discrimination and heartless acts shown by the human race. I have also learned that if one does not choose to take a stand against what one believes is wrong, then he or she is just as guilty as the persecutors. Although I am not a warship or a battle tank, and I cannot always protect him from the abusive language or violent attacks, I know I am his friend and he is mine. It is because of him that I choose to act for what is morally right and not socially just. The value of a human life is far more significant than the importance of one's reputation. Aristotle once said, "For without friends no one would choose to live, though he had all other goods."

Book Review: *Holes,* By Louis Sachar

~By Elizabeth Schultz
Eighth grade, Evergreen Jr. High School
Veradale, Washington

My opinion of the book *Holes,* by Louis Sachar is that it is an outstanding piece of literature. Rated on a scale of one to ten, I would give it a ten.

I thought that the most interesting part of the book was how there were three stories going on all at once. This gave the book an extra spark that captured and held my interest throughout the entire story.

There is the story of Stanley Yelnats IV who was teased so much that he would walk home from school instead of riding the bus. Stanley learns about his family's history and goes through some positive changes during a summer at Camp Green Lake.

"Kissin' Kate Barlow" was an eighteenth century outlaw who had a "deadly" kiss and a lot of lipstick. Kate knew Stanley's great-grandfather and gave him a trouble that followed through to the next generation.

Stanley's "no-good-dirty-rotten-pig-stealing-great-great-grandfather" was involved in a story of a stream that flowed uphill, a gypsy, and a curse that was placed on him and all of his descendants.

I would recommend this story for all ages. My older sister, seventeen, gave Holes to me when she was finished reading it. Then I passed the book on to my younger sister when she was only ten. She absolutely fell in love with the story after the first time she read it. It's a book that can be read over and over. I have read it four times!

I would like to leave you with my absolute favorite element of the entire story, the ending. Now, I am not going to actually tell you what happens, but I am going to give you a very important piece of advice. Throughout the entire story you must stay aware of what is happening, or the ending may be a little bit fuzzy. Personally, I had to read it a couple times to understand how the ending even happened, let alone trying to put all the connections together.

Movie Review: The Historical Accuracy of *Spartacus*

~By Megan Yarmuth
Tenth grade, Trinity Preparatory School
Orlando, Florida

Although the meaning of *Spartacus* is quite grand, the plot is quite simple; a fictional account of a slave rebellion in Ancient Rome during 73-71 B.C. Because there is flimsy evidence on Rome and Roman opinions, it was a great risk to make a film based on such loosely based facts. Although the director, Stanley Kubrick, did a phenomenal job, credit is also due to Howard Fast, whose book was the inspiration for the film.

Not only was *Spartacus* recognized by the 1960 Academy Awards and the Golden Globes, it was hailed by critics and audiences everywhere. Who would be surprised by that? *Spartacus* was, and still very well may be, the most historically true picture ever produced. Every detail from language to wardrobe is precise. With an ensemble cast including Kirk Douglas, Jean Simmons, and Laurence Olivier this picture was destined to be a classic from the get-go. *Spartacus* pulled in $13 million dollars at the box office in its first year running.

The picture brilliantly expresses the time period and the lives of slaves and gladiators alike. The accuracy of the wardrobe earned costume designers, Peruzzi, Valles, and Bill Thomas, Academy Awards. Their use of color and texture for each of the character's clothes added to the feel of the picture, and represented the experience or stature that the character had achieved. Despite the fact that *Spartacus* was only filmed in a 167–day stretch, Kubrick still achieved full accuracy. Everything from the opening shot in Death Valley to the battle scenes in Spain were spectacular. Even the values of Roman society are captured. This is a large risk to present to your audience. If the way of life in Ancient Rome is too risqué or extreme the audience will feel overwhelmed or confused. Kubrick presents Roman opinions in a subtle, more "PG-13" way.

Although *Spartacus* is an extremely accurate film overall, it is virtually impossible to find a film with no flaws. *Spartacus* has some flaws, but nothing too major to take away the audience's enjoyment of the film. For example, the lack of the "SPQR" tattoo was the first mistake I happened to notice. Not regarding the truth of the film, there are scenes that might not be visually appealing to a general audience. One instance is the Roman use of crucifixion, although this is a historically accurate method of execution, to a modern audience this could be interpreted as an offensive mocking of Jesus.

There is no way someone could argue that this isn't one of the best films ever put into production. It is a genuine look at life through someone else's eyes. For 185 minutes, we can see how someone else lives. This picture is trying to tell its audience that sometimes we have to fight for things we believe in, even if the consequence is death. *Braveheart* is basically an adaptation of *Spartacus*. The main character, William Wallace is an exact parallel to Spartacus. He leads his people with one objective at mind—Freedom. Both heroes' stories end fatally, but they fight for their conviction, and never give up. Kubrick is telling his audience to "Never give up." This is a typical, and most misrepresented theme in films today. It is a rarity to find a film that expresses it so well.

Contributors

Information about the student authors and artists.

The biographies of the students have undoubtedly changed since their work originally appeared in Student Bylines Magazine (2000–2002), but these brief comments may still add depth to the writing and artwork that is included in this anthology.

Beckie Acree enjoys writing stories, drawing and singing. She is a member of a girl's barbershop singing group. Her many pets take up the rest of her time. Reflections of Summer was painted in watercolor. Americana Lilies and Scarlet Potentilla were created in colored pencil.

Kim Adams is an aspiring young woman who plans to achieve a career in the medical field. A graduate of Mead High School, she is attending the University of Washington and participates in the Honors Program. Holding pride in her African-American background, Kim encourages people to celebrate diversity by appreciating our differences and recognizing our similarities as a culture.

Corey Anderson likes to draw wildlife and landscapes in his free time. He likes scratchboards and painting with acrylics.

Ben Barnhill enjoys drawing, running, and playing baseball.

Julie Baxter likes horses, bike riding, video games, and swimming.

Liz Blodgett loves acting and writing. She considers herself a very spiritual person.
Liz is involved in drama and the Creative Writing Club at Ferris. Liz dedicates "Rude Awakenings" to every author who thought they could get away with cheap 'n' easy style.

Madeline Blodgett likes to struggle with the guitar and play the piano.

Erica Broadwell likes to hang out with friends and she is very involved at school. Participation in a leadership class helps her accomplish her involvement at school.

Michelle Bronny enjoys writing poetry and has used this form of expression to help in dealing with her father's death.

Katy Brukardt enjoys art, literature, and playing the violin.

Briana Bryant enjoys reading and writing. She lives in Thailand and loves playing soccer with her friends. Briana's inspiration for her entry was thinking about life and what it means to her.

Isabel Cattadoris likes athletics. Her drawing was inspired from a photo.

Christy enjoys reading mystery books and likes watching television and movies.

Lee Ciavola enjoys rock climbing, snowboarding, and skateboarding.

Alex Ciurlionis is an eighth grader from New Zealand. He likes to read, write, and play video games.

Nick Clevenshire loves to read and write poetry. He likes to ride his bike during his free-time.

K. Clough likes to read and play basketball. She wants to attend classes at Washington State University to be a veterinarian.

Hector Comacho loves to draw, watch TV, and is very proud of his Mexican heritage.

Jesse Cummins was born in Missoula, Montana. He has enlisted in the Army and will travel to Georgia shortly after graduation. He will go into Microwave Systems Operations and hopes to get a job at a communications company after his tour of duty.

Laura Dailey's interests include creative writing, drama, gymnastics, and music. Her sense of humor adds to the fun she shares with friends and family.

Zach De Young likes drawing and sports. His drawing was sketched in pencil.

Olivia Pearl Distler likes art, biking, and chilling with her pals. Her artwork was created in pastels.

Brandan Drake enjoys the outdoors and riding four wheelers. Brandan likes to draw and hopes to be a graphic designer.

Taylor Edmonds enjoys building model cars. He also likes to draw cars and trucks in his free time.

Elo V. Elwell is eleven years old and likes bicycling, skiing, and soccer. He also enjoys art.

Beau Ferderer is an avid hockey player. Beau has enjoyed art since he was two years old.

Alex Fern enjoys working, listening to jazz, rock climbing, and cooking.

Caleb Garrison likes football and soccer. He also likes to draw. Caleb draws in every spare minute he has. His drawing was sketched in pencil.

Tina Green is an art lover and Christ follower. She hopes to finish high school, move on to college, and have a family. Tina's inspiration for her black and white watercolor painting was the Twin Tower bombing.

Matt Greer is a Senior at North Central High School. He plans to attend the University of Washington in the fall.

Vitaliy Grishko is interested in many different things: computers, cars, music, movies, reading, sports, the outdoors, and church. His inspiration for this illustration was from his enthusiasm for cars.

Stephanie Guerra is a creative wild-child who loves to play her guitar and using her computer.

Lauren Hatcher has an interest in drama, writing, and the Internet. She plans to attend college as a Drama major, Creative Writing minor, and become a professional theatrical stage manager.

Gregory Hein enjoys playing baseball and football. He wants to become a lawyer.

S. Jackson likes to do gymnastics, run track and hangout with friends.

Cecelia Jerow spends time working with her horses. She also enjoys drawing and taking photos of her family and animals.

Caroline Stephanie Kraft wants to be a therapist. She likes soccer and cats.

Lindsey Kropp enjoys reading, hanging out with her friends, and has future writing aspirations.

Jennifer Leader enjoys drawing and painting. She is a cheerleader and is involved in other various clubs. She would like to attend San Diego State University.

Ashley M. Lessmeier likes horses and enjoys drawing them. She spends time in Montana riding horseback.

Rachel Marie Lewis loves old mopars, wildlife, and being a teenager. She enjoys writing because it's a great way to express oneself.

Justina Long enjoys swimming, hanging out with friends, and playing basketball and softball. She enjoys writing poems also.

Mellisa Lelia Lowe is one of eight children. She loves her church and enjoys playing the cello.

Jessica Mann is considering a career in either engineering or law enforcement and is an avid fan of drawing and writing.

Shannon McDonnell is active in yearbook, sports, safety patrol, and is recognized for leadership abilities. She enjoys being with friends, reading, camping, and traveling.

Lissy Metlow, who likes to ski and swim, is twelve and a half years old.

Suzanne Miller enjoys reading and writing. She lives in a forested area where wild animals are commonplace. She is a graduate of D.A.R.E.—Drug Abuse Resistance Education.

Andrew Morgan has been experimenting with various forms of art for several years—both at home and at school. Andrew hopes to major in art at college.

Jennifer Norman loves to play softball as both a pitcher and first baseman. Jennifer's favorite medium to work with is scratchboard.

Kim Olsen enjoys reading, painting, theatre and hangin' out with friends. Her painting is done in watercolor.

Crystal Orcutt intends to become either a counselor or social worker. She hopes to publish a novel and a collection of her poetry and artwork sometime in the future.

Dan Peterson likes to play baseball, football, and video games. Dan is currently reading *Fight Club* by Chuck Palahniuk.

Sarah Peterson likes paintball, movies, and reading. Sarah is currently reading *The Portable Henry Rollins*.

Katie Peterschick likes volleyball, track and enjoys hanging out with her friends.

David Porter is a talented artist who creates and draws from the heart. Instead of becoming angry and bitter over his father's death, David has chosen to honor his father by drawing and showing his work with others.

R. Randolph likes to read, write, and listen to music.

In his spare time, **Julian Redman** enjoys reading, writing, and studying stars. He also wants to become an astronaut and go to school at Harvard University.

Gavin Rhodehouse likes to associate with all kinds of people. He loves all media of artwork, as well as girls. He likes to be involved in any activity that involves interacting with others.

Gaelen Sayres is in the 7th grade and he likes to run, draw, fold origami, and do gymnastics in his spare time.

Anna Marie Schaefer loves art, cooking, sewing, and reading. She studies piano, cello and ballet.

Elizabeth Schultz loves traveling and running. Her favorite sport is track. Elizabeth has six sisters.

Katie Schultz enjoys many forms of artistic expression. The painting, Zebra, was done in watercolor.

Twinkle Schutt was raised in Spokane. She enjoys writing, playing her guitar, and country music.

Jocelyn Selle enjoys drama, ballet, and art. Writing is a hobby she enjoys. Her inspiration is a picture in her mind.

Mica Smith's hobbies include writing (poems & short stories mainly) as well as drawing.

Cory Taff likes to play football and enjoys spending time with his friends.

Priscilla Thompson has wanted to be an author since she was in second grade. She also likes to read and draw. Priscilla has a younger brother and sister.

Jomayra Ivette Torres enjoys reading and writing poetry. Her hobbies include playing sports and collecting stamps.

Jeremy Trimble is an ambitious student. His love for writing is what drives his existence.

Ileana Varnam likes to write. She dreams of one day publishing a novel.

Shawna Vincent recently visited Yellowstone National Park and found many interesting subjects to photograph. In addition to enjoying photography, Shawna is learning to play the clarinet.

Michelle Vinje was born in Indonesia and recently went on a trip there with her family. Her photograph was taken in Kuta Beach, Bali. Michelle enjoys traveling and being with her friends.

Divya Vishwanath has beautiful black hair, and a mean tennis serve. She is a loving person and enjoys piano, school, writing, reading, sports, and being with her family.

Kelly Warner enjoys running, rock climbing, and kayaking.

Stephanie Wells likes to write and play sports such as track, volleyball, and tennis. She also enjoys school and being with friends.

Jane Westrick likes to draw, play soccer, take pictures with her digital camera, and hang out with friends.

August Wyssman plans on attending the University of Nebraska's College of Journalism and Mass Communication in 2002 to earn her M.A. in News—Editorial and Journalism studies. August's favorite movie is "Singin' In The Rain" because she enjoys Gene Kelly. Although she likes a few modern movies, August prefers an old musical any day.
The subject of *Ode to a Furball* is her eight-week-old Cocker Spaniel puppy named June Bug.

Megan Yarmuth is a student in Winter Park, Florida. Her aspirations are to one day become a producer/director of her own feature film. Megan plans to attend New York University and major in film and photography.

Yekaterina Yangolenko has blue eyes and blond hair. She loves to sing, write poems, short stories, and take photographs. She always has a big smile on her face and is ready to learn something new.

0-595-27133-2